CLASSIC

JOURNEY To The CENTRE Of The EARTH

RETOLD BY
PENNY DOLAN

ILLUSTRATED BY
PAUL DAVIDSON

EDGE FRANKLIN WATTS

LONDON · SYDNEY

First published in 2011 by
Franklin Watts
338 Euston Road
London NW1 3BH

Franklin Watts Australia
Level 17/207 Kent Street
Sydney NSW 2000

Text © Franklin Watts 2011
Illustrations by Paul Davidson © Franklin Watts 2011
Cover design by Peter Scoulding

A CIP catalogue record for this book
is available from the British Library.

ISBN 978 1 4451 0459 1

Dewey Classification: 823.'9'2

1 3 5 7 9 10 8 6 4 2

Picture a
Gennad

Contents

Chapter One
An ancient message

A journey to the centre of the Earth?
An impossible idea, yet that was where
we went!

Our adventure began in May 1863 in
Hamburg, Germany, where I lived with my
uncle, the great Professor Otto Lidenbrock.

I was working at home on my uncle's
collection of rocks and minerals when my
uncle rushed in. He was holding a dusty
old book that he had found in a second-
hand bookshop.

"Axel, look at this. A fascinating ancient
history of Iceland!"

As he opened the book's cover, a grubby
piece of old parchment fluttered out and
landed on the ground. My uncle snatched
it up and unfolded it. He peered closely at
the writing.

The letters looked like small black twigs lying on snow. I couldn't understand a single word.

"What are they, Uncle Otto?"

"Old Icelandic runes. They're from an ancient Scandinavian alphabet. I should be able to read them easily. But first I want to know who was the last owner of this book." He reached for his magnifying glass and peered at a dark smudge inside the cover.

"Incredible! Arne Saknussemm, alchemist and explorer. He wrote this message two hundred years ago."

My uncle was most excited. "Get a pen and some ink, boy. Write down every word as I translate it."

I waited, but he did not speak.

"Bother! It's all in code," he raged. "This will take some time."

Slowly, he began to translate. As he read the letters out, I wrote them across a sheet of paper. Then I wrote them in lists down the paper. Then I wrote them backwards. No clue jumped out at us.

"This code is impossible!" my uncle roared, storming out of the room.

I worked on quietly. I grouped the letters together in new ways. Frightening words appeared: *ice, anger, cruel, sacred wood, sea.* Suddenly I felt faint.

I flapped the pages in front of my face to cool myself. As the sheets blurred together,

I saw two words quite clearly: *crater, earth*. What did this dreadful writing mean?

I soon decoded the whole parchment. My heart sank. The message could send my uncle on a journey from which he might not return.

I was about to throw it all into the fire when my uncle returned. As I handed the sheets over, my face showed I knew the secret.

"Tell me, Axel," he ordered.

So I read out the terrible words:

"Descend into the crater of Snaefell Volcano before the new moon rises in July. Wait until the shadow of the mountain appears in the volcano. At noon the shadow will mark the passage that leads..." I hesitated.

"Go on!" shouted my uncle.

"To the centre of the Earth."

My uncle laughed and leaped madly around the room.

"Well done, Axel! But what we need now is dinner." He rang for Martha our cook.

The dinner was indeed delicious. I was just taking a second slice of apple pie when my uncle jumped to his feet.

"Oh, do hurry up, Axel!" he snapped. "There's no time to waste. I'm off to town to order all we need."

I gasped.

"You pack our trunks, boy. It's already May, and we must reach Iceland by July. We leave the day after tomorrow!"

Glumly I finished what was to be my last good dinner for a long time.

Chapter Two
To Iceland!

By the next day, the garden was full of equipment. There were ice axes, climbing crampons, rope ladders, torches, water bottles and much more.

I tried my best to stop my uncle.

"Perhaps the parchment's a hoax?"

"I don't think so, Axel."

"What if Snaefell explodes?"

"It's an extinct volcano. Hasn't exploded for centuries."

There was just no way I could stop him.

Our coach, loaded with luggage, set off at dawn. We went by steamship and train to Copenhagen, where we booked tickets for Iceland. A ship was sailing in five days' time.

We sailed to the Icelandic port of
Reykjavik. My poor uncle was so seasick he
stayed in his cabin most of the time. I went
up on deck and watched the whales and
porpoises swim past. At last, I saw Iceland
appear on the horizon.

Our guide in Iceland was a tall Icelander called Hans. He had bright eyes and fair shoulder-length hair. He was a man of few words, and usually answered my uncle by nodding or shaking his head.

We bought new equipment. We had thermometers, firearms and gunpowder, hiking boots, a first aid kit and three water bottles. We also took some electric lanterns.

"We can melt snow for drinking water," my uncle decided. "And I'm sure we'll find plenty once we're underground."

My uncle hired four sturdy Icelandic ponies. They were so small that my uncle's feet almost touched the ground. We rode two of them and the other pair carried our equipment. Hans strode beside us over the bleak, tree-less landscape.

Within a week, we were camped at the foot of Snaefell. The next day we said farewell to our faithful ponies, and began the steep climb up the volcano.

The path was stony and slippery. We were
glad when we reached the smooth, solid lava
further up the volcano. Above the snowline
it was bitterly cold but we could not stop.
A windstorm was heading our way.

"Hurry, hurry!" shouted Hans. "Up!"

Chapter Three
Into the crater

We scrambled under a ledge of rock and the storm passed below us. Although it was midnight, it was still light. The sun does not set during the Icelandic summer.

The next day, we reached the rim of the crater. We roped ourselves together. Then we descended into the bowl of thunder and flame. As we reached the floor, I looked back up at the perfect disc of sky. Would we ever return?

Suddenly my uncle shouted with joy. He pointed to a nearby rock with marks carved into it.

"Look at those letters Axel. A.S. *Arne Saknussemm.* He stood on this very spot!"

Three tunnels yawned open at our feet. Which was the one true passage? We needed the sun, but the sky was covered in thick grey clouds. Sleet and rain fell from above, and no sun shone.

"It will be too late soon!" my uncle raged.

At last, on the fifth day, the sun shone out in glory. At midday the shadow of the peak fell across the crater, sharp as a knife. It struck the middle tunnel.

"Onward," cried my uncle, rising to his feet, "to the centre of the Earth!"

As I leaned over the tunnel, my hair stood on end with fear. I started to sway. Hans' strong arms pulled me back to safety.

"Careful!" he said.

We tied the most fragile equipment to our packs. My uncle carried the measuring instruments. Hans took the tools. I carried our firearms.

Hans wrapped everything else up in a blanket. He tied the bundle with rope and flung it down the shaft.

"We'll collect it at the bottom," my uncle decided.

Then we began our slow descent. We looped a long rope around a jutting rock. Then, one by one, we grasped both ends. Slowly we descended to a lower ledge. Then we tugged the rope down, and began again. It grew darker all the time. Stones tumbled down around us on all sides. At last we reached the bottom.

"Halt!" Hans said.

We ate dried meat and biscuits. Then we curled up in our blankets. As I lay there, the crater above me looked like a giant telescope. I gazed up at the single bright star overhead.

A ray of sunshine woke us. It filled the rocks with sparkling crystals. We ate, put on our packs, and fixed on our electric lanterns.

I took one last look at the sky far above us and wondered if I would ever see daylight again. Then we entered the dark tunnel.

My uncle's watch told us the time. When evening came, I was tired and thirsty.

"Uncle Otto, there's no water here," I said.

"We'll find some in the next layer of rock. Do stop worrying, Axel."

We travelled on and on. Suddenly the tunnel split in two. Which path should we take?

My uncle checked his instruments. "Left," he said.

We entered a high cavern. Broken seashells crunched under our boots. Then the roof of the passage grew lower. We crawled through rocks printed with fossilised plants and ferns. Still there were no springs or streams.

"We've got three days' water left," I said.

"Then ration yourself, Axel," my uncle answered briskly. "Onward!"

Chapter Four
Water!

The rocks changed as we descended. We saw stone full of small fossils and seams of dark coal. We became too thirsty to speak. Then, on the fifth day, we faced solid rock.

"We took the wrong path," my uncle growled. "We must go back."

"Uncle, I can't." I fell to the floor.

"Get to your feet, Axel! We are running out of water. We are not running out of courage," he raged.

We went back. The heat was unbearable and soon all my water was gone. When we reached the fork, I fainted.

I woke to find my uncle leaning over me.

"Here. I saved these last drops of water for you, my brave boy."

I drank thankfully. "Are we going home now, Uncle?"

He looked at me tenderly. "Poor boy! Hans

can take you back. I shall carry on the quest alone."

"No, you must come back too!" I begged.

My uncle's eyes twinkled. "No, Axel. While you were sleeping, I explored the right-hand tunnel. It leads downwards. I'm sure we'll find water there. All is not lost."

My spirits rose. "Then I will come with you," I cried, so on we went.

A day came when we knew we had gone too far. We could not return alive. Our strength faded and we sank to the floor.

Dimly, I spied Hans pick up his lantern and move off down the tunnel. "Is he deserting us?" I thought, dropping asleep.

Soon, Hans woke us. "Water, water!" He put his hand behind his ear.

We hurried down the tunnel. Yes, we could hear water flowing in the tunnel walls all around us. But the tunnel itself was totally dry. Solid rock kept us from the gushing water. What could we do?

Hans smiled. He lifted his pick-axe and struck the wall. A jet of boiling water spurted from the rocks. "Ouch!" he cried.

The water soon cooled down. We drank deeply and filled our bottles. The water streamed along the tunnel ahead of us.

"Water flows downwards," said my uncle. "If we follow it, we will reach our goal. Well done, Hans! I name this stream the Hansbrook after you."

After some days, the stream tumbled down a deep chasm.

"We'll descend by rope," said my uncle.

Below the waterfall was a vast grotto. We spent a day resting there. Then we carried on with our journey, day after day, until something terrible happened.

Chapter Five
The Lidenbrock Sea

I was walking ahead, daydreaming.
Suddenly, I realised I was alone. I turned. I
couldn't see Hans or Uncle Otto anywhere.

Perhaps I had walked too fast? I hurried
back but saw nobody. I was by myself and
my lantern was dimming.

I tried to pull myself together. After all, I
had water in my bottle and three days' food.

I tried to find my way. Soon I was lost
among the dark passages. I stumbled and fell
unconscious to the floor.

A loud noise woke me. I heard rocks
falling and human voices. I yelled for help.

"Axel!" came a distant voice. "Is that you?"

"Yes, Uncle," I cried.

"Listen, my boy. We are in a cavern
somewhere below you. Keep going. I'm sure
you will end up here. See you soon, Axel."

"See you soon, dear Uncle!"

How awful it felt to leave the sound of my uncle's voice again!

On I went for several days. Then the tunnel sloped rapidly. It sent me scrambling down a steep shaft. I hit my head against some hard rock and passed out.

I came to in my uncle's arms.

"He's alive!" Uncle Otto and Hans smiled down at me. I drifted into sleep again.

Much later, I woke. I heard the sound of waves breaking on a shore.

"Am I dreaming?" I asked.

My uncle smiled. "No. We are beside an underground sea, nephew. Just rest."

How could I rest? I stumbled outside and saw a vast shining ocean.

"Behold the Lidenbrock Sea, Axel!" my uncle declared.

As soon as I felt stronger, Uncle Otto and I explored the strange seashore. There were forests of gigantic mushrooms, huge ferns and strange spiny trees.

"Look!" I cried. On the ground lay a huge bone. "The jaw of a mastodon!" The sands were scattered with skeletons of prehistoric animals. "How did it get here?"

My uncle looked at the bone in wonder. Then he shook his head. "Not everything can be explained, Axel."

Hans chopped up some fallen tree trunks. We roped the logs together and made a fine raft. The fossilised trunks were light enough to float but far stronger than stone. A single trunk was our mast. A large blanket became the sail.

We set off. The wind was quite strong so the raft sped along. We rested and gazed around us. Hans dropped a fishing line into the water. He caught several strange eyeless fish for our supper.

My uncle was busy scribbling notes about the Lidenbrock Sea. "How deep is the water here, Hans?" he asked.

Hans tied an iron axe to a long rope and

dropped it into the waves. It did not even touch the bottom. He hauled the axe back up. To our horror, the metal had been marked by two giant teeth.

Huge ripples broke the glassy surface of the sea. Something was swimming towards us.

Whatever had Hans disturbed?

Chapter Six
A prehistoric battle

The sea around us swirled and churned wildly. We looked at each other in alarm. Then two terrible dinosaurs rose from the waves. One, a huge ichthyosaurus, was like a monstrous porpoise. The other, with a neck longer and thicker than any serpent, was a plesiosaurus. Both gigantic creatures were circling around dangerously close to our tiny raft.

As Hans and my uncle struggled to stop our raft turning over, I rose unsteadily to my feet and reached for a gun. I held the rifle ready, but Hans signalled not to fire. The snarling creatures did not want us. They were locked in their own deadly battle.

I could barely believe what I was seeing. The monsters fought fiercely, whirling around us. Our little raft was tossed to and fro and we clung on for our lives.

At last the dinosaurs plunged down again into the deep water.

The water calmed. Then the lifeless body of the plesiosaurus floated to the surface.

Luckily, the wind blew us onward before the victor could return for us.

After some days on the raft, we heard roaring water. We spotted a low shape in the sea. Then a great spout of water rose high into the air. Were we going to be drowned by a gigantic whale?

Hans climbed the mast to get a better view.

"Geyser!" he shouted cheerfully.

It was a small rocky island with many pools of bubbling mud. Every so often, a geyser sent water high into the air.

"I name this place Axel Island," my uncle announced.

As we left Axel Island behind, an electrical storm began. Dark clouds rolled around us. Thunder crashed. Lightning flashed. Hailstones hammered down. The wind was deafening. For hours my uncle and I clung to the raft. Hans steered us bravely on. Every hair on his head was tipped with light.

Finally, on the third day of the storm, a great ball of lightning smashed our mast and sail. We drifted helplessly towards a reef of jagged rocks.

As the raft crashed against the shore, Hans grabbed me to safety.

We fell on the scorching sand, rain pouring down on our bodies.

The weather was calm when I woke. Hans was already setting our belongings out to dry. We had a few food supplies, and could fill bottles with rainwater from puddles. Although our guns were gone, we still had a small barrel of gunpowder.

"I wish I knew where we were," said my uncle. "My compass seems wrong. The needle should point north. I think it is pointing south."

Hans was busy repairing the raft, so we went exploring. We clambered over long ridges of lava and came to a beach scattered with prehistoric bones.

My uncle studied one skeleton after another.

Then he gasped. At his feet was a giant human skull. There was the body of a giant human close by. Perfectly preserved, it had wrinkled skin and a fine head of hair. Its teeth were strong, and its toenails were like long claws. The creature stared at us through empty eyes. Many more bodies and bones were spread along the sands.

"Remarkable!" said my uncle. "However did such beings get here?"

As we walked on, we entered a dark, gloomy forest, full of huge trees. Crystal streams bubbled between rare mosses and massive ferns.

Suddenly, we heard a tree crash to the ground close by.

My uncle grabbed my shoulder.

"Mastodons!" he whispered.

Ahead was a herd of gigantic prehistoric elephants. They were uprooting trees with their enormous tusks. My uncle edged closer to them.

"Wait!" I told him. "We are unarmed. No one could face them."

But I was wrong.

A creature twice the size of any man moved among the mastodons. His hairy head was as big as a buffalo's. He was herding the mastodons with a huge branch. As we stood there spellbound, he turned towards us. We fled as fast as we could back to the safety of the shore.

Chapter Seven
An explosion!

Scattered around the seashore were many rocky headlands. I was sure that I'd seen them before.

"Have we sailed round in a circle, Uncle Otto?"

"The only way to find out is to look for our footprints."

That was how I found the ancient dagger buried in the sand. No caveman could have owned such a weapon.

"The steel blade has been broken. It's been used for carving stone, Axel."

"Uncle," I said, "the dagger pointed towards those cliffs."

There, close to a narrow tunnel hidden between two rocks, we discovered the explorer's initials: *A.S. Arne Saknussemm.*

I lost all fear. "Onward!" I shouted, darting into the tunnel in excitement.

"Not yet, Axel," my uncle decided. "We must plan. Let's go back to Hans and bring the raft round to this beach."

Full of hope, we sailed the raft across the bay. Our lantern showed a gigantic boulder was blocking the tunnel. Was this the way?

"Saknussemm was here centuries ago," I cried. "Perhaps there's been an earthquake since then? Surely we can move the rock, can't we?"

"Gunpowder!" said my uncle.

Hans chipped a hole in the huge boulder and filled it with guncotton. Meanwhile, we laid the gunpowder in a long fuse.

"Ready?" I shouted.

But my uncle refused. "Not yet, Axel. This will need all our strength. We go tomorrow."

I do not know how I slept that night.

In the morning, we decided to wait offshore. I lit the long fuse, and raced back to the raft. We pushed the raft out into the bay and sat waiting. Ten minutes passed.

I do not recall any explosion, but I saw the cliffs bulge out and part like curtains. Then the whole shore disappeared.

The sea turned into one colossal wave. We clung on desperately as the raft rose. Then we were sucked down into a dark, endless cavern. Day after day, the raft whirled around, faster than any train. Only Hans' calm face, lit by the lantern, gave me hope.

Everything was washed away, except for the rope that coiled round the broken mast. Most of our food was gone, but we were more likely to drown than starve. Great torrents of water fell, choking us. We gulped down air whenever we could.

Then the whirlpool changed direction.

"Aha! As I thought," said my uncle. "The water has found its own level. Now it is rising and taking us up with it."

"Where to?"

"I don't know, nephew," he said with the strangest smile. "But there's no point in worrying. We might die. We might live. Let us finish the food and get ready to face whatever happens."

Chapter Eight
End of the journey

We ate, and sat lost in our own thoughts. We could die at any minute.

Then the rocks shook. The water rose. The air grew so hot that we threw off our jackets. The water around the raft began to boil. Were we going to die here in a white-hot furnace?

"We are lost, Uncle," I cried. "We are caught in an earthquake."

"You are mistaken, dear nephew." He smiled. "I'm expecting something much better than that. We are in the chimney of another volcano. How fortunate!"

"Fortunate?" I screamed.

"Indeed. The water has almost boiled away. Soon our raft will be rising on the molten lava."

"Lava?" I shouted.

"Keep calm, Axel. It's our only chance of reaching the surface again."

My uncle was absolutely right.

We waited. The raft rose higher and higher. Days passed. Still we ascended. Where on Earth could this mountain be?

Then everything stopped. Our raft did not move. After fifteen minutes or so, we started rising once more. This happened many times.

"What's going on?" I asked.

"Simple. The volcano stops for breath now and again. Our time will come soon, Axel."

It came indeed, but I have no clear memory of what happened. I remember loud explosions and roaring flames. I remember the raft bobbing about wildly on the lava, and a wind far stronger than any hurricane rushing us along, faster and faster.

I woke on a steep mountainside. Hans grabbed me quickly in case I rolled back into the crater. My uncle was sitting there, looking about. We were almost unhurt.

"Are we in Iceland?" I asked.

Hans shook his head. "No!"

There were no snowy wastes here. A fierce sun was baking our skin. Below us were trees, orchards and vineyards. Away in the distance was a pretty little harbour where fishing boats bobbed on a blue sea.

However our volcano still threw lava into the air now and again. It was time to move, and we were dying from thirst.

At the foot of the volcano's slopes we came to a cluster of cool olive trees and springs of fresh bubbling water. A young goat-herd wandered towards us.

"What is this mountain?" my uncle asked.

The goat-herd shook his head.

My uncle tried one language after another.

"Stromboli! Stromboli, Italy," the boy shouted, and ran off.

What a journey we had made! Snaefell. Stromboli. We had gone into the mouth of one volcano. We had come out of another a thousand miles away. We had reached the shores of the Mediterranean Sea. It was unbelievable! Though we had not reached the centre of the Earth itself, we had ventured further than any other explorer, apart from Arne Saknussem.

Our appearance soon attracted a crowd of local people. We told them that we had been shipwrecked. They cared for us until we recovered.

We got back home to Hamburg safely. Our cook, Martha, was full of delight. She had told everyone about our expedition. Tales of our journey spread far and wide, and the mayor of the city gave a great feast in our honour.

At last the day came for farewells. Our brave friend Hans went back to Iceland. My uncle, Professor Otto Lidenbrock, went back to teaching at the University.

As for me, I have been writing this story. On my desk is Uncle Otto's old compass, with its needle pointing south. It was changed forever by the storms we three travellers faced, deep down in the centre of the Earth.

Jules Verne (1828–1905)

Jules Verne was born in France on 8 February 1828. He was fascinated by exploration from an early age, and once tried to stow away on a boat to the Caribbean!

Jules Verne

Verne's other lifelong passions were science and writing. At school, he started writing short stories that explored all of his great loves – quirky tales of adventurous journeys, that were rich in geographic and scientific detail. On leaving school however, his family encouraged him to follow a more stable career, and Verne trained as a lawyer.

Verne combined writing with the law for a while, but soon tired of it and decided to devote himself to his writing. In 1863, he finally published his first novel – a story about balloon exploration in Africa. Many other celebrated works, including *Journey to the Centre of the Earth*, soon followed.

Over a hundred years after his death, Verne is still one of the most popular and most translated authors in the world. He is often hailed as the father of science fiction, for he had the gift of making science accessible to all in his writing.

Journey to the Centre of the Earth (1864)

Journey to the Centre of the Earth was partly inspired by a book published by Charles Lyell, a famous geologist, in 1863, which explored the age of the human race. Verne used Lyell's findings as a basis from which to describe to readers what the prehistoric world was like, stretching from the ice ages to the dinosaurs. He also created a classic adventure story, which has been made into a TV series, films and even a theme park ride!

Titles in the CLASSICS RETOLD series:

978 1 4451 0461 4 pb
978 1 4451 0818 6 eBook

978 1 4451 0460 7 pb
978 1 4451 0815 5 eBook

978 1 4451 0458 4 pb
978 1 4451 0819 3 eBook

978 1 4451 0462 1 pb
978 1 4451 0817 9 eBook

978 1 4451 0459 1 pb
978 1 4451 0816 2 eBook

978 1 4451 0457 7 pb
978 1 4451 0820 9 eBook